The Looking Down Game

BY LEIGH DEAN

illustrated by Paul Giovanopoulos

The Looking Down Game

fW FUNK & WAGNALLS, NEW YORK

For David

Text copyright © 1968 by Leigh Dean.
Illustrations copyright © 1968 by Paul Giovanopoulos.
First published in the United States of America,
1968, by Funk & Wagnalls,
A Division of Reader's Digest Books, Inc.
Library of Congress Catalog Card Number: 68-13075.
Designed by Ben Birnbaum
Printed in the United States of America.
1

IT WAS LATE AT NIGHT. Edgar lay in bed, his eyes wide open. No matter how hard he tried, he could not go to sleep. He had never slept in this room before. And a neon sign across the street filled it with blinking light. Edgar hated first nights in strange places. It seemed he was always moving.

Grownups didn't care.

"One block is just like another," his mother told him.

"The park is close. You can ice skate there. Play ball. Row a boat on the lake," his dad told him.

"You'll soon make new friends," Aunt Alice told him.

Edgar wished everything grownups said were true. But he knew it sometimes wasn't so. He'd only moved two blocks to the left, and one block to the right, but it would be ages before he felt he belonged here. It was like that in cities. Edgar was seven and had lived in a city all his life.

At last he fell asleep thinking about next fall when he would go to another new school, where there would be more strange rooms and many strange faces.

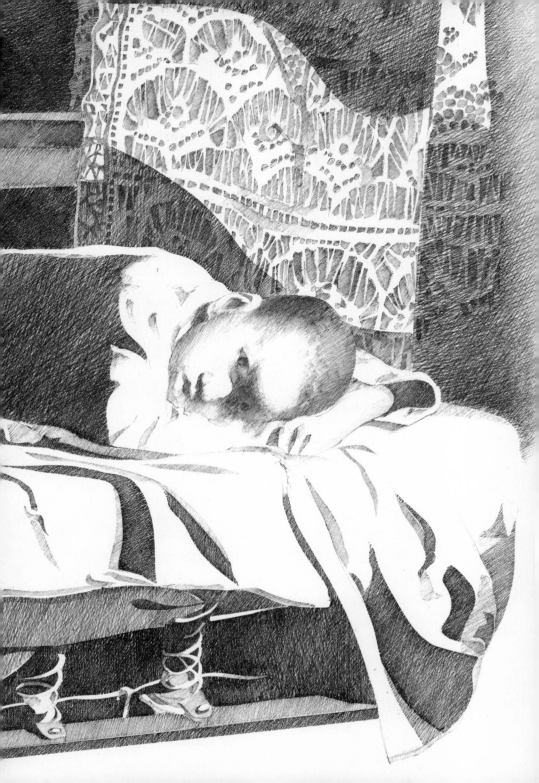

The next day Edgar went exploring along his new block. One vegetable store, a small, green newsstand, a shoeshine shop, a meat market with sawdust on the floor, a fish market where a fat orange cat slept against the windowpane in the sun, and a small, dark candy store.

12

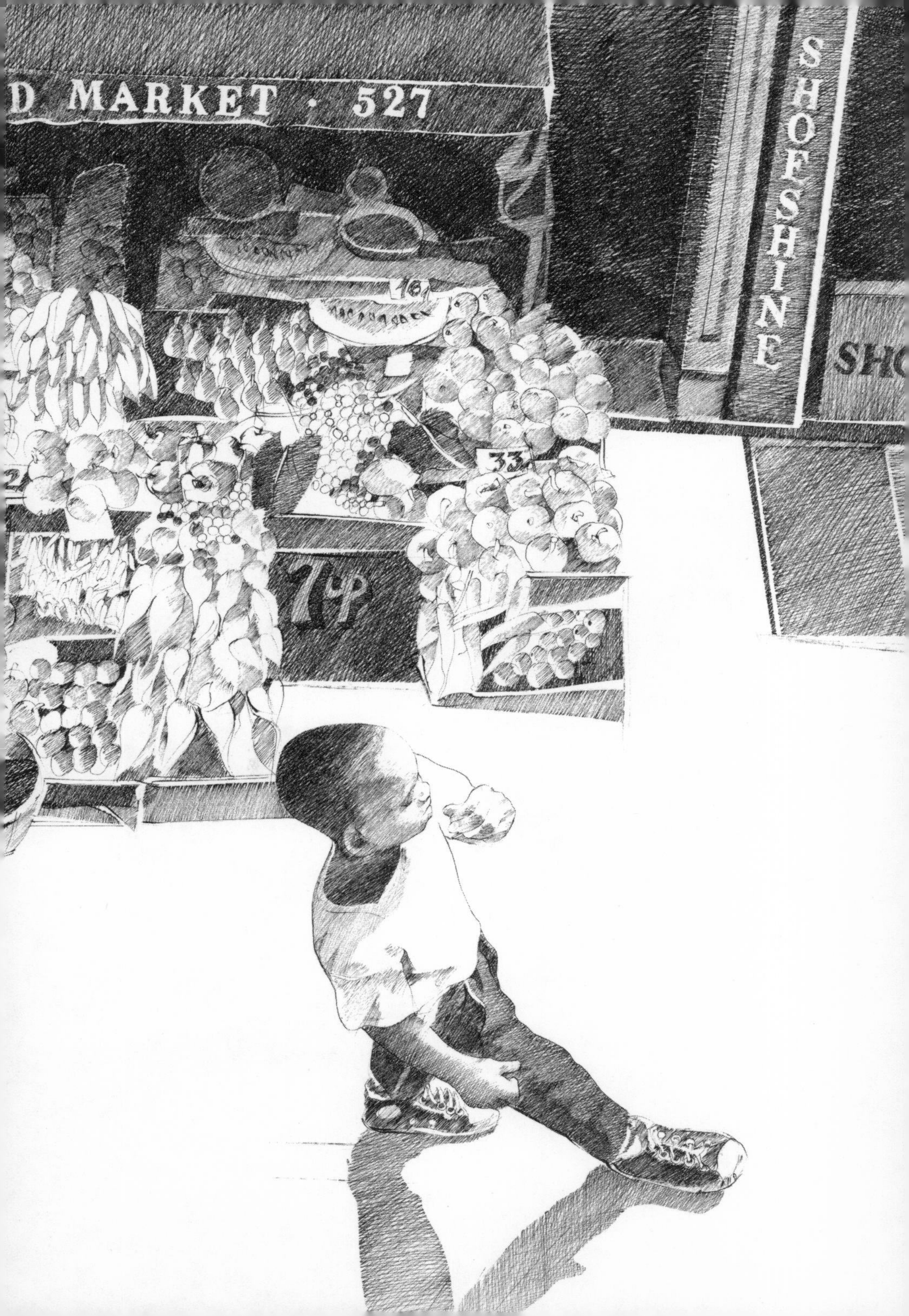
D MARKET · 527
SHOESHINE
SHO
33
7¢

At the end of the block and across the street was the park. Edgar waited for the green light; then he crossed. The grass smelled sweet, a little like raw carrots, and it was soft to walk on. Some kids were tossing a football around. Edgar watched it spiral back and forth until it dropped near where he stood. A boy came running. Edgar wondered if he would be in his class in September. The boy grabbed the ball, then looked up. Edgar felt suddenly shy and looked down—and there, crawling slowly over his sneaker was a big, shiny black bug. It was the biggest, most beautiful beetle Edgar had ever seen. He picked it up carefully, put it into his cap and started home.

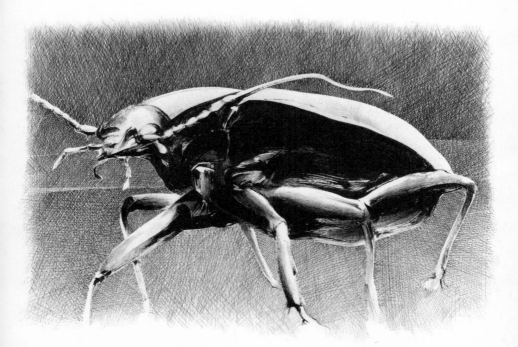

On the way, Edgar practiced walking along the
narrow curbstone near the gutter. He looked down,
straight down, to see where his feet were going—and
there, right in front of his toe was a long, white and
blue feather. It was clean—and straight—and perfect. Edgar picked it up carefully and put it into his
cap to keep it safe.

Then he did some thinking. He took a peek at the
beetle and at the long, perfect feather and thought
about other surprises he might find if he looked

straight down. Then he grinned, gave a shout and
swung around a parking meter. Here was a game, a
secret looking down game he could play all by himself. He could play it every day and make a collection
of things he saw straight down.

In the early summer, after a heavy rain, Edgar sloshed through muddy puddles and stared into clear pools of water catching upside down pictures of trees, buildings, and his own face. He would squat at the curb and watch gum wrappers, bits of paper and cigarettes float quickly by and tumble into the sewer; or he'd stand under a store awning that dripped and watch the spotted backs of ladies' stockings as they passed. Sometimes, he would sail his toy boat in the stream by the curb. But he always had to race to save the boat before the sewer could swallow it.

In the fall, on his way to school, Edgar would watch the wind turn umbrellas inside out and blow men's hats off and hide them under cars. Strong winds could make him trot when he tried to walk.

They were the best kind. When he got tired, Edgar would just sit still and count the leaves on the sidewalk: five red ones, three yellow ones, and many brown ones. Too many brown leaves to count.

One day, along a shortcut through the park, Edgar looked straight down and found a bird's nest. He had never seen one close up. It was made of thin twigs, string, and grass, all woven together. Edgar cupped it easily in the palms of his hands and took it to school.

"Hi, Edgar."

"Hi, Tory."

"Hi, Melvin. Hi, Tory. Hi, Edgar, what have you got there?" asked Sandy.

"A bird's nest," said Edgar.

"Gee," said the others, "let's see."

Edgar opened out the palms of his hands and they all had a look.

When Miss Leuwen called the class to order, she asked Edgar if she might borrow the bird's nest. Then, the whole class spent the morning talking about birds and nest-building.

Soon winter came and Edgar got up early in the morning and crunch, crunch, crunched through the snow. He tracked the fresh prints of squirrels, birds, and a very big cat. He even found the imprint of a "snow angel" resting in a circle of shrubs. At the end of the block was a huge snowdrift. To climb over it Edgar had to take large, sinking steps. He felt his feet slip into the snow and watched the tops of his boots disappear deep into the drift. Each step left behind a dark, warm tunnel that waited for another pair of boots.

Then, at school, Edgar liked the look of all those boots leaning together higglety-pigglety on the wet cloakroom floor. There were zipper boots, lace-up boots, fur-lined boots, and black, flappy galoshes with five metal buckles that went click, click, click. One day, after school let out, Edgar followed a pair of galoshes out the door and down the street, left-right, left-right, until he heard a strange, cracking sound. He stopped and listened. The cracking sound grew louder. Then down, down shot a giant icicle *thump* into the snow. When icicles began to fall, Edgar knew the days were getting warmer. He tried to remember the feel of hot sunshine as he sucked the cold icicle.

Spring came and Edgar wiggled his toes in the warm dancing patches of sunlight and felt the air in his classroom grow heavier and heavier with the approach of summer's heat. Each day Edgar examined the new grass blades that had pushed their way up between spaces in the sidewalk. He collected popsicle sticks and peanut shells. The peanut shells became families that lived in square popsicle houses. On really warm days, Edgar took a stick and drew lines in the soft, bubbly tar. Sometimes, the stick gathered enough tar to make a small hard ball that didn't bounce.

One afternoon, Edgar sat on the brick steps of his building rolling a tar ball between his hands. As he rolled it, getting it perfectly round and smooth, he looked down and saw a very little ant pulling a very large fly. The ant tugged and tugged at the fly's head. Then it ran around to push and push the fly from behind. Edgar followed the direction the ant was going—and there, by the side of his building, was a little hill of dried dirt. Out of a hole at the top of the hill came other ants busily carrying more grains of dirt. Edgar looked back at the little ant with the large fly. The ant had a long way to go, and the fly was very large, so Edgar picked up the ant and the fly and put them down near the hole in the hill of dirt. The little ant ran around in circles inspecting the fly. Then it waved its feelers and two more ants came out of the ant hole to help. Together they pushed and pulled, tugged and dragged the fly up the hill, then down, down into the hole.

Time had passed quickly and the shadows on the sidewalk bobbed in big, dark patches. The air had turned cool and Edgar got up to go inside. *I like watching ants*, he thought. Then he had an idea. He would catch a fly every day and leave it by their hole.

School ended and summer came and Edgar had the

whole of every day to himself. Games of jacks and marbles and jump-rope tick, tick, ticked along the block, while roller skates rumbled over the pavement, back and forth, back and forth. The black asphalt grew hot in the sun, so hot it made one's feet burn. Edgar left his block and crossed to the soft, cool grass and shady park. He followed a dog with droopy ears and a lolling tongue. The dog was going to the park, too. Together they walked beside the wall until they came to a space in the stone where a path led into the park. Edgar entered the park, took five steps, and stopped.

There, at his feet, were a trillion pigeons and a trillion pieces of corn. Which way should he go? Edgar tried to go around the pigeons on the left side, but a boy peddling fast on a bike was coming up that way. He tried to go around the pigeons on the right side, but a mother with twins carrying balloons scattered the pigeons on that side. *Well*, thought Edgar, *it's through the middle*. And he looked straight down, held his breath and marched quickly through the mass of birds. The pigeons fluttered, took to the air as he passed, then one by one settled down again to pick and peck at the corn kernels.

Edgar was so busy looking straight down, holding

his breath and marching quickly that he swerved off
the path. *CLUNK!* went his head as he hit something
hard. "Ouch," said Edgar and looked up. Straight up
into the eyes of a boy his size perched on a thick limb
of an oak tree high above his head.

"Hi," said the boy.

"Hi," said Edgar.

"Come on up," said the boy and beckoned.

"It's high," said Edgar and he stepped back to measure the distance. His head thrown back, Edgar followed the rough, gray tree trunk up to the lowest spread of fat branches and on up to the thickets of thinner branches covered with flat, green leaves that crowned the top and seemed to reach almost to the sky.

"Give me your hand, I'll help," said the boy. All at once, more than anything else, Edgar wanted to climb this tree. He had never climbed a tree before. He would climb this tree and find out what being up was like.

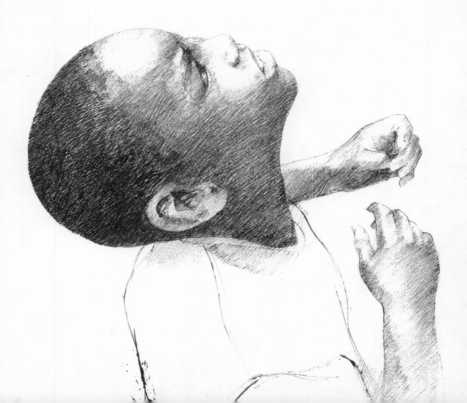